PENELOPE JANE

A Fairy's Tale

BY ROSANNE CASH

ILLUSTRATED BY G. BRIAN KARAS

JOANNA COTLER BOOKS

An Imprint of HarperCollinsPublishers

Library of Congress Cataloging-in-Publication Data
Cash, Rosanne.
    Penelope Jane : a fairy's tale / by Rosanne Cash ; illustrated by G. Brian Karas.
        p.   cm.
    "Joanna Cotler Books."
    Summary: Penelope Jane, a spunky fairy whose mischievous behavior causes chaos in the classroom, uses some quick
thinking and a song to save the school from a fire. Includes lyrics and music.
    ISBN 0-06-027543-X
    [1. Fairies—Fiction.   2. Schools—Fiction.   3. Fires—Fiction.] I. Karas, G. Brian, ill.   II. Title.
PZ8.3.C273Pe   2000   98-41512
[E]—dc21   CIP
                                                       AC

Typography by Alicia Mikles 1 2 3 4 5 6 7 8 9 10 ❖ First Edition

For Caitlin, Chelsea, Baby Jake, and especially Carrie, who insisted that
Penelope Jane be liberated from her bedroom and into the world at large
—R.C.

To Elizabeth
—G.B.K.

Tall as an eyelash, quick as a plane
was the tiniest fairy, Penelope Jane.

Penelope Jane was a five-year-old fairy,
and her very best friend was five-year-old Carrie.
She lived with her mother, Jeannette de la Fesser,
in the top right-hand drawer of young Carrie's dresser.

These fairies were French,
and they just loved to eat.
Seven *croissants*
was their favorite treat.

Never fly into a sliding glass door.

Never drink milk that has spilled on the floor.

Always remember to dry *both* your wings.

And when eating croissants, try not to sing.

Penelope went to the smallest of schools,
where she learned to sing songs and obey Fairy Rules.

Like . . .

Never fly into a sliding glass door.

Never drink milk that has spilled on the floor.

Always remember to dry *both* your wings.

And when eating *croissants*, try not to sing.

One day when Carrie was skipping to school,
she felt on her shoulder a droplet of drool.

"Penelope, what are you trying to do?
My school is too big for a fairy like you."
"Oh, please let me come," cried the stowaway fairy.
"I'll be *perfectement* . . ."
"Do you promise?"
said Carrie.

But Penelope wasn't *quite* perfect that day.

She did *quite* a few things that went wrong in some way.

She dive-bombed the turtle.

She pestered the fish.

She logrolled the chalk.
She danced in a dish.
She fell in the glue,
got Miss Lilly Pott flustered.
Got stuck in a sandwich and covered with mustard.

Finally the teacher said, "You are a pain!
Go sit in the corner, Penelope Jane!"
Our wild little fairy felt sorry and sad.
She slunk to the corner; she knew she'd been bad.

The children marched out, calling, "Lunchtime! Let's go!"
And P.J. was left all alone, but—OH NO!!!

At first she smelled smoke, then she saw a small flame.
She flew to the window and called Carrie's name.

She pulled the alarm bell with all of her might—
but it was too heavy and she was too light.

And then she remembered a wonderful song
her mother had written, called "How to Be Strong."
She let her voice fly—Boy! Could that fairy sing—
Then she figured out just how to make that bell ring. . . .

PULL DOWN

LOCAL
FIRE
ALARM

CRAFTS

BRRiiiNGGG G

BRRiiNG

BRRiiiiNG

BRRriiiNG

PULL DOWN

LOCAL FIRE ALARM

BRRiiNG

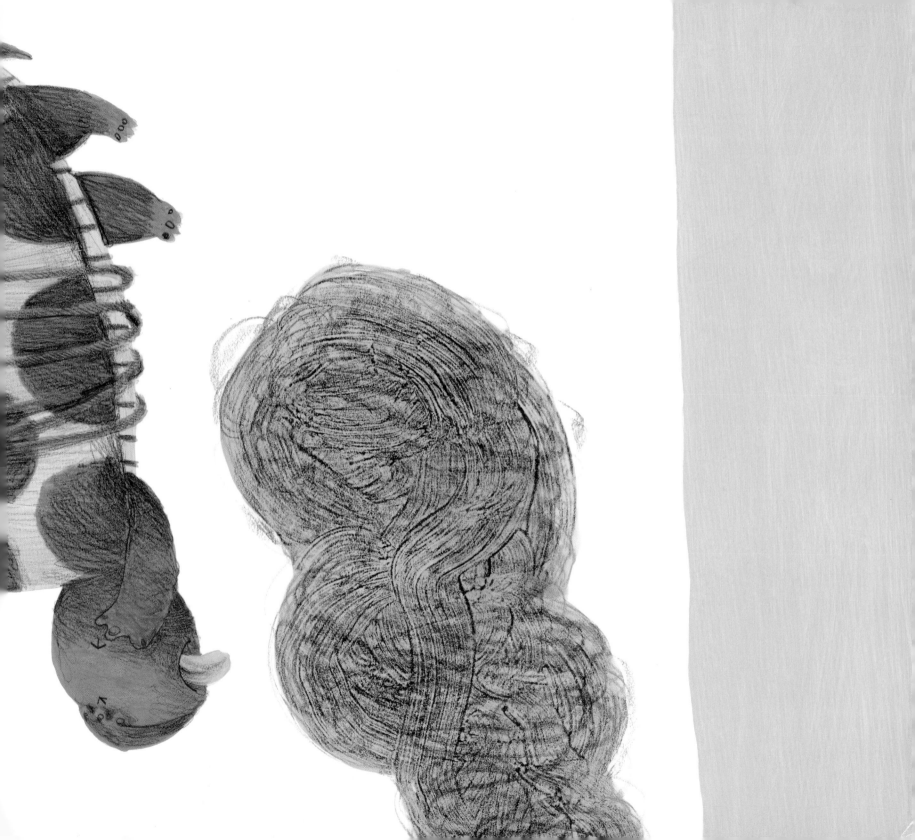

"Penelope Jane, you're a hero!" cried Carrie.
"No trouble at all," said the eyelash-high fairy.
"You sure saved the day, can you come back next week?"
Penelope laughed, and she kissed Carrie's cheek.

The school had a party, a big celebration.
They gave Mr. Turtle a month-long vacation.

Penelope's mom baked a thousand *croissants* and handed them out at the press *conference*.

That night in their home—
Carrie's room, P.J.'s drawer—
they ate and they sang 'til they sank to the floor.

They tucked into bed and they turned out the lights,
and Penelope whispered her seven good nights.
As Carrie lay snug in her soft cozy bed,
she looked at Penelope Jane and she said,
"I really would like to learn how to be strong."
And P.J. said, "Carrie, I'll teach you my song."

How to Be Strong

VERSE:

YOU WAKE UP IN THE MORNING SO SMALL AND SWEET

SAY BONJOUR AND GO   BUT YOU STAND UP TALL TO EV-'RY

ONE YOU MEET   AND LET THEM KNOW YOU KNOW

CHORUS:

HOW TO BE STRONG WHEN THE WORLD IS ROUGH   AND

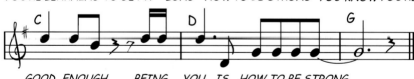

YOU'RE LEARNING TO GET A- LONG HOW TO BE STRONG YOU KNOW YOU'RE

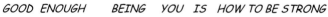

GOOD ENOUGH   BEING   YOU IS HOW TO BE STRONG

If you're in a jam, just take a breath
Dry both wings and fly
You can get some great ideas
Though you are eyelash high

Chorus

Well, you might be a lonesome bird
Who travels 'round the world
You might be a king or a queen
Or a little French fairy girl

You wake up in the morning, so small and sweet
'Cause that's just who you are
And even with those little feet
You can travel far.

Chorus

Fairy Facts

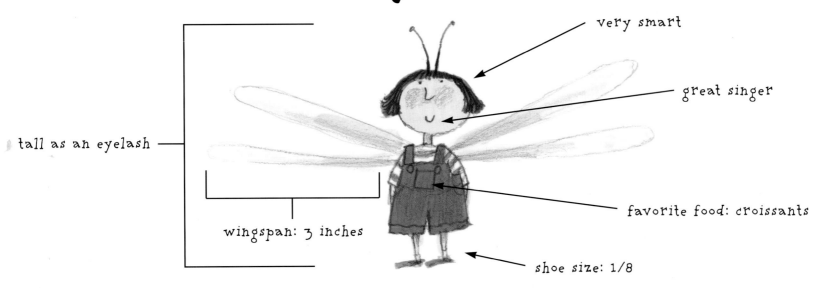

very smart

great singer

tall as an eyelash

favorite food: croissants

wingspan: 3 inches

shoe size: 1/8

longest flight without a rest: 27 feet

most *croissants* eaten at one sitting: 31

age at first solo flight: 18 months

favorite subject in school: singing

How Penelope Jane got her name:

Penelope's father, Pen de la Fesser, and her mother were equally proud of their English and French lineage—which dated all the way back to the Middle Ages—so they wanted their daughter to have a name that was from both sides. So Pen and Jeannette named their baby daughter Penelope Jane de la Fesser. ("Jane" because Jeannette just liked the name.) Unfortunately, Pen and Jeannette divorced, but remain very good friends. Pen still lives in France, where Penelope visits him every summer, but Jeannette and Penelope moved to New York City when Penelope was three years old, because Jeannette got a great job offer in a Fairy Bakery.